Pearl

THE MAGICAL UNICORN

SALLY ODGERS   ILLUSTRATED BY ADELE K THOMAS

FEIWEL AND FRIENDS ♥ NEW YORK

For Imogen, and in memory of Kyalas,
my very first unicorn —SALLY ODGERS

To Maik, Mum, and Dad, thank you for all your
support and encouragement. —ADELE K THOMAS

A FEIWEL AND FRIENDS BOOK
An imprint of Macmillan Publishing Group, LLC
120 Broadway, New York, NY 10271

PEARL THE MAGICAL UNICORN. Text copyright © 2018 by Sally Odgers. Illustrations copyright
© 2018 by Adele K Thomas. All rights reserved. Printed in China by RR Donnelley Asia Printing
Solutions Ltd., Dongguan City, Guangdong Province.

Our books may be purchased in bulk for promotional, educational, or business use.
Please contact your local bookseller or the Macmillan Corporate and
Premium Sales Department at (800) 221-7945 ext. 5442 or by email at
MacmillanSpecialMarkets@macmillan.com.

Library of Congress Control Number: 2019940849
ISBN 978-1-250-23550-3 (hardcover) / ISBN 978-1-250-23551-0 (ebook)

Feiwel and Friends logo designed by Filomena Tuosto

Originally published in 2018 in Australia by Scholastic Australia under the title
Pearl the Magical Unicorn.

First US edition, 2020

10 9 8 7 6 5 4 3 2 1

mackids.com

Chapter 1

Pearl the unicorn felt full of sunshine as she pranced down to the pond. It was a magical morning and she had the coolest idea ever.

She was going to use her magic to make crunchy apples appear! She wanted to share them with her best friends in the whole, wide Kingdom, Tweet and Olive.

Her friend Tweet was a firebird. She was small and fast and loved to play tricks, even if they weren't really funny.

HA! HA! HA!

Her friend Olive was an ogre. She was strong and brave and she loved to eat. She once ate an entire bowl of tomato soup, including the bowl!

Both of her best friends absolutely loved apples. Even more than Pearl did.

"Flying flapjacks!" said Pearl. "I can't wait to begin. Let's see . . . ," she muttered. "How does the magic go? Toss-wiggle-wiggle? I'm sure that's right. Here goes!"

She tossed her head and
wiggled. A puff of pink
sparkles exploded
into the air.

Then a giant pink teddy bear fell from the sky!

"Oops," said Pearl. "That's not an apple! But maybe Olive will like it anyway. I'll try toss-toss-wiggle!"

She tossed her head twice and wiggled.

A shower of bright pink buttons fell on
top of her.

"Oops. Oh, why can't I get it to work?" asked Pearl with a stamp of her hoof. She shook herself free of the buttons. "Come on, magic! I want to make some apples!"

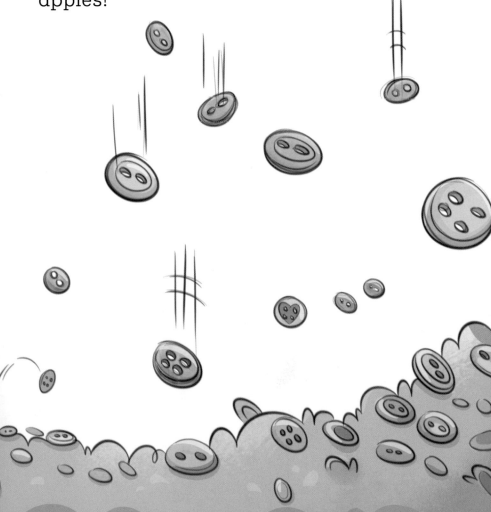

She was about to try again when something tugged her tail.

Pearl jumped high in the air. **"Hopping hats!** It's a gobble-un!" she cried.

When Pearl landed on the ground, she looked around. But nobody was there!

Then something tugged her tail again.

TUG-TUG.

"It's two gobble-uns!" she gasped.
Pearl looked under her. But again
nobody was there.

TUG-TUG-TUG.

"Great goats!" Pearl threw her front hooves in the air. "Three of them! Go away, gobble-uns, or I'll turn you into frogs!"

She looked to her right.

She looked to her left.

TUG-TUG-TUG-TUG.

"Purple potatoes! Help!" Pearl spun around on the spot, swishing her tail with a SNAP!

Something small and orange spun through the air and bounced behind the teddy bear.

"Ha, ha! Tricked you!" it said.

It wasn't four gobble-uns after all. It was Pearl's friend Tweet the firebird.

"**Bouncing bananas**, Tweet! I almost turned you into a frog!"

Tweet flapped her wings. "Not gobble-un! I'm Tweet!"

Pearl laughed. "I can see that. Guess what, Tweet?"

"What?"

"I'm going to make a crunchy treat for you and Olive."

"With magic?" Tweet asked.

Pearl nodded.

"No!" Tweet squawked. "No magic! No magic! No-no-none!"

"Why not?"

"Pink feathers!" Tweet exclaimed, and tossed her crest. "Remember?"

Pearl remembered the time she tried
to give Tweet a magical makeover.
Her feathers had turned pink . . . and
then fallen out. Poor Tweet had to wait
until they grew back. She had hated
being bald.

Suddenly there was a stomping noise from behind them.

"Gobble-un!" cried Tweet, spinning around.

"It's me, silly." Their friend Olive the ogre walked over to them. She picked a pink dandelion from the meadow and tucked it into her hair.

"Hi, Olive!" Pearl and Tweet said together.

"I'm just about to make apples appear," said Pearl.

"Yum!" Olive replied, licking her lips.

Pearl tossed, wiggled, and tossed. There was a puff of pink sparkles.

Then Olive suddenly cried out, "Ouch!"

Chapter 2

Olive held up the flower that she had put in her hair. It looked . . . different. It was still pink and it still had petals, but now the flower had a body, four legs, a swishing tail, and a face with beady eyes.

The three friends stared down at a very small lion.

"That's definitely not an apple," Pearl said, shocked.

The lion gave a tiny roar and shook its
mane of petals.

"You must have made it with your
magic," said Olive. "Pearl, you made
a teeny, tiny, bitey flower lion."

"Oops," Pearl said. She was just trying
to make an apple appear! How had she
turned Olive's flower into a lion?

The lion looked up at them grumpily.

"I don't think it's happy with you," said
Olive. "And it bit my ear."

27

"Ooh!" Tweet flew down. "Bad lion!" she squawked.

The lion roared. Tweet jumped back and fell over. "Awwwk!"

Pearl looked at the lion again. Olive was right. It did look grumpy.

"Cold crumpets!
I'm never going to learn
how to use my magic,"
said Pearl sadly. "I've
been trying to get it right
all morning."

"You can do it, Pearl,"
Olive said. "And even if you can't,
you're our best friend and we love you.
Right, Tweet?"

"Right!" Tweet squawked.

"Think about all the other things you
are good at," Olive said.

"You laugh at my tricks!" Tweet said.

"You're kind and you always cheer us up," Olive added. "And you're the nicest unicorn in the whole Kingdom."

"I'm the only unicorn in the Kingdom."

Then the lion sprang down from Olive's hand, roared, and turned back into a pink dandelion.

"You're the best unicorn in the Kingdom," said Olive.

"The very best!" said Tweet.

"I don't know," said Pearl. It was still a magical day, but somehow she felt less full of sunshine. What if she made something else by mistake? Something *dangerous* . . . like a dragon?

"Come on, Pearl," Olive said, grinning.
"You can't just give up!"

Pearl looked at Tweet and Olive, unsure.
They smiled at her. Maybe her friends
were right. She didn't really want to
give up. She wanted to magic up some
apples! And she felt as if she could do it.
She just needed to try harder.

"Okay, get ready for some apples!"
Pearl said happily.

"Yay!" cheered
Olive and Tweet.

"Now, is it toss-wiggle-toss-prance?
Or . . . Oh, I remember!" Pearl tossed her
head and wiggled.

Toss-toss-wiggle-wiggle-TOSS!

For a second, Pearl thought nothing would happen, and then there was a loud SPLAT as a wave of strawberry milk fell from the sky! It hit Tweet, covering her from beak to talon in pink milk.

"Awwwk!" squawked Tweet, dripping.

Olive stared at her. Then she giggled.
She laughed and laughed, pointing at
Tweet completely covered in pink milk.

"Oops," said Pearl. "I can fix it!" Quickly, she tried to undo her magic.

Toss-toss-wiggle-wiggle-TOSS!

With a loud SLOP, more milk fell from the sky, this time landing right on top of Olive's head! Olive was dripping and pink, just like Tweet. It was Tweet's turn to laugh.

Pearl knew she could fix it. What if she tried the magic backward?

TOSS-wiggle-wiggle-toss-toss went Pearl.

There was silence in the meadow. Pearl looked around. She had done it! There was no more pink milk!

Then, with a giant SPLOSH, a big wave of pink milk fell right on top of Pearl.

Chapter 3

Pearl, Olive, and Tweet jumped into the pond to clean themselves. Tweet splashed around in the shallows, squirting Olive with water.

Olive scooped up a big handful of water and splashed it over the firebird.

"Awwwk!" cried Tweet.

On the other side of the pond,
Pearl sat down and moped.

Olive and Tweet stopped playing. "Come on, Pearl, it was pretty funny. I've never seen so much strawberry milk before in my life!" said Olive.

"I wasn't trying to make strawberry milk. I was trying to make *apples*."

Olive sat down and put her arm around Pearl.

Tweet flew up from the pond and perched on Pearl's head, hugging her.

"Don't worry, Pearl," said Olive. "You're good at so many other things!"

"Yes! Yes!" Tweet chirped.

"What if instead of milk, it had been a huge, enormous, giant strawberry?" said Pearl.

"Yum! I love strawberries," said Olive.

"What if it had landed on Tweet?"

"Awwwk!" Tweet squawked in horror. She peered up at the sky, just in case a giant strawberry was coming her way.

"Oh." For once, Olive looked serious. "No, that wouldn't be good."

"Pink parakeets! That would be horrible!" Pearl sighed. "That's it," she said. "I've made up my mind. I am never going to do magic again."

Her friends stared at her.

"But, Pearl," Olive said. "You can't stop doing magic."

"No!" squawked Tweet.

"I can stop if I want to," Pearl said. "At least until I can get it right!"

"But you're Pearl, the magical unicorn! Magic is part of who *you* are, just like loving food is part of who *I* am. You can't just . . . stop," said Olive.

"Sizzling salad! I can and I will. From now on, I'm not magical Pearl. I'm just plain Pearl."

There was a pause. Olive and Tweet looked at each other, unsure.

"What now?" Tweet asked.

"Um . . ." Olive frowned. "I know! We
can get something to eat. I'm hungry!"

"Good idea," said Tweet.

"You're always hungry," Pearl said.

"Ogres need food," Olive reminded her. "We're big and we're strong and we eat lots." She picked up a pine cone and bit off a chunk.

CRUNCH!

"Yummy?" asked Tweet.

"Not very," said Olive. But she took another bite anyway.

"Where should we go?" Pearl asked.

Olive thought hard. Then her eyes went wide. "My big brother told me he saw a huge apple tree absolutely loaded with apples!"

"Lolloping lemons!" cried Pearl. "We love apples!" She felt better already. "Why didn't you say something earlier?"

Olive shrugged. "I forgot. Anyway, this tree is a long way from here."

"Where? Where?" Tweet bounced around with excitement.

"Way inside the Wandering Forest," said Olive.

"Jumping jelly! I can get us there in a jiffy," Pearl said. "Let's go!"

Olive scrambled onto Pearl's back with Tweet, and the three friends set off toward the Wandering Forest.

Chapter 4

Pearl, Olive, and Tweet trotted
through the meadow until they came
to a long line of tall toadstools blocking
their path.

"Uh-oh," said Olive.

Stamp-stamp-jiggle-shake!
Pearl was about to make the toadstools disappear when she remembered something. She wasn't magical Pearl anymore. She was just plain Pearl.

"Hold on!" she said to her friends. She took a flying leap and jumped over the toadstools in their way.

"Whee!" cried Tweet.

But on the other side of the toadstools there was a long, muddy stream. Pearl's hooves landed in a big pile of mud.

SPLOSH!

"Oops!"

Olive giggled. "Your legs look like they've been dipped in chocolate. I love chocolate."

Hoppity-toss-jiggle-toss! Pearl was about to do magic to clean her chocolate legs when she remembered that she wasn't magical Pearl anymore. She was just plain Pearl.

Instead she carried her friends safely across the stream. Soon they turned down a track between two high hills.

The path went on through the trees, and then the three friends entered a darker part of the forest.

"Olive, are you sure this is the way?" Pearl asked.

"I hope so," Olive said. She lifted her head and sniffed the air with her ogre nose.

SNIFF!

SNIFF!

"Fee-fi . . . yes, I smell apples in the distance."

Pearl stepped between the trees and stumbled over a branch. Flickety-toss! She was about to make her horn glow with light so they could see. But then she remembered she was just plain Pearl.

CRACK!

Pearl stopped. What was that? There was something behind them.

"Gobble-un?" squawked Tweet.

"Of course not," Olive said.

Pearl looked over her shoulder. What if it *was* a gobble-un? Just a little flickety-toss and she'd be able to see. But then she remembered that she was trying to be just plain Pearl. **Shivering snakes**, thought Pearl. **Being just plain Pearl is harder than making magic!**

Pearl, Olive, and Tweet trotted on
through the dark forest, until Olive
suddenly cried out,

"STOP!"

Pearl stopped. **"Pickled plums!** What is it?"

"Nothing, silly," Olive said. "We've gotten to where we were going. The apple tree is over in that clearing." She slid down from Pearl's back. "Oh, yum! My big brother was right."

They all stared at the apple tree. It was huge. It was enormous. It was absolutely covered with big, juicy apples.

"Apples!" squawked Tweet, flying into the air with excitement.

"Chomping cheese!"

exclaimed Pearl, looking up at the huge apple tree. "That's the biggest tree I've ever seen!"

"All right," said Olive. "Let's eat!"

There was a silence. Then Pearl asked, "How are we going to get them off the tree?"

"Pick them, of course," said Olive in surprise. She stepped up to the tree,

stood on her ogre
toes, and reached up with her
ogre arm.

"Um."

"Dripping dumplings,
Olive," said Pearl. "You can't reach."

"I can so reach," huffed Olive.
"I'm an ogre! Ogres can
always reach food."
She stretched up as
high as she could,
but she couldn't
reach the apples.

"My turn!" Tweet flew up into the tree and perched there, staring smugly down. "One, two, or three?"

"Lots," Pearl said. She was really hungry after all that trotting.

"Yeah! Lots!" said Olive.

Tweet marched along a branch to a fat, juicy apple. It was bigger than she was. Tweet gave the apple a poke with her beak. It hardly moved at all.

"Um."

"**Trembling tomatoes**, Tweet!" said Pearl. "You can't do it, either."

"Can so." There was a pause while Tweet stared at the apple. "Can't," she admitted.

"You try, Pearl,"
said Olive.

How would just plain Pearl get those apples off the tree?

Chapter 5

Plain Pearl leaped in the air. She
kicked up her hind legs. She jumped
as high as she could. But she couldn't
reach the apples.

Then Pearl had an idea. "Shake the tree," she said to Olive. "I'll catch them as they fall."

Olive got hold of the tree trunk and shook it with her ogre strength. The tree shook and shuddered.

An apple fell. Pearl sprang and caught the apple on her horn.

"Yay!" she called. Down came another and another, and Pearl caught each one. "Yum!"

There was just one problem. The apples were stacked on Pearl's horn like marshmallows on a stick.

She jumped in the air and bounced around. The apples stayed stuck to her horn.

"I'll pull them off," offered Olive.

Olive grabbed the apple stack. She pulled and pulled, but the apples stayed stuck to Pearl's horn.

"Tap-dancing turnips!" said Pearl grumpily. "I can see the apples. I can smell the apples. I just can't eat the apples."

"Maybe you should try just a teensy bit of magic?" suggested Olive.

Then Pearl had another idea. She jumped high in the air and whipped her head sideways.

WHEEEEE!

The apples flew off, shot through the
air, and sailed right into the mouth of . . .
a cave.

"Oops!" said Pearl.

Tweet and Olive peered into the darkness
of the cave.

"It looks creepy and it smells bad," said Olive, holding her nose.

"Gobble-uns?" suggested Tweet.

"Probably bats," Olive said.

"I'm going to get those apples," Pearl said bravely.

Flickety-toss! Pearl was about to do a little spell for light when she remembered she wasn't magical Pearl anymore. She was just plain Pearl.

She made her way slowly into the cave. **Angry anteaters!** It was dark. And Olive was right. Something smelled bad. Pearl sniffed some more. She caught a whiff of apple.

Olive and Tweet followed Pearl into the cave.

Pearl put her head down and poked
around with her horn. No apples.
But what was that? Someone was
munching. Someone was talking.

"Is that you munching, Olive?"
whispered Pearl.

"No," Olive whispered behind her.
"Is that you talking, Tweet?"

"Not me!"

Pearl and her friends
crept forward.

They heard more munching. They heard more crunching. Someone was talking in a rough and grumpy voice.

" . . . and then we'll march right into the Kingdom."

"Yay!" cheered a voice.

"These squishy apples are yucky," said another.

The voices were coming from farther inside the cave.

Pearl, Tweet, and Olive sneaked forward and peeped around the corner.

Sitting hunched around a small, smoky fire were three big gobble-uns!

Chapter 6

The light flickered on the gobble-uns' sharp, grumpy faces and their long, twitchy fingers.

Pearl saw that one of them was eating an apple.

"Oh! Oh! Oh!" said Tweet in a scared whisper.

"Let's get out of here," hissed Olive. She was a brave ogre, but *no one* went near gobble-uns if they could help it.

"Wait," Pearl said.
"They've got our apples."

They watched as the nastiest-looking gobble-un wiggled its crooked fingers.

"We're gonna march right through the Kingdom doing stinky magic!"

"Yayyyy!" cheered the gobble-uns. "Stinky magic!"

"We'll take over and rule the world!"

"And gobble up all the tasty apples."

95

"What's stinky—" Olive stopped short as a wave of the most horrible stink drifted through the cave.

Tweet's eyes rolled back and she
fell off Olive's shoulder.

Olive picked her up and Tweet's eyes
fluttered open again.

Pearl choked as another wave of terrible stink shot out. **Fizzing fish!** It was horrible!

"Help . . . ," said Olive worriedly. "I'm gonna . . . I'm gonna . . . AH-AH-AH-CHOO!" roared Olive in a big, loud sneeze.

It echoed around the cave.

There was a second's pause and then they heard a gobble-un call out, "What was that?"

Quickly, Pearl pushed everyone out of sight.

"Someone's in the cave," said one of the gobble-uns.

"Let's get 'em," said another gobble-un.

"And gobble 'em up with tasty apples," said the third gobble-un.

Toddling toads! Pearl did not like the sound of being gobbled up by gobble-uns!

They heard the creatures stomping
toward them.

Pearl tried to think. What to do? Her
nose tickled with the smell of the stinky
magic. It was getting worse as the
gobble-uns got closer.

"Pearl!" squealed Tweet. "Do your magic!"

"I'm plain Pearl."

"We need magical Pearl!" choked Olive. "Quick!"

"You can do it," Tweet said.

"You're our best friend and you never let us down," added Olive.

Could she really do it? She did
like being magical Pearl. Maybe it
didn't matter that her magic wasn't
perfect all the time. And her friends
needed her.

The gobble-uns raced
around the corner and
spotted them.

"It's a horse, a flying fish, and
a green cat! Let's get 'em!"

"Now!" cried Tweet.

Another wave of stinky magic almost knocked Pearl down.

Terrible tutus! If only the gobble-uns weren't so stinky!

Toss-toss-toss-wiggle-toss! That should do it. Pearl tossed three times, but just as she was about to wiggle, she breathed in another wave of stinky magic!

"AH-AH-AH . . ."

Chapter 7

". . . CHOOOO!"

Pearl sneezed! Right in the middle of her magic!

There was a pink puff of sparkles and then cries from the three gobble-uns.

"Yuck! Get it off me!"

"Erk! Gah!"

"Ick! I'm gonna be sick!"

Then Olive gasped and Tweet squealed with laughter.

"Look! Look! Pink!" cried Tweet.

Pearl opened her eyes. In front of her, dancing around in disgust, were the three horrible gobble-uns with filthy hair, stinky feet, and . . .

. . . bright pink tutus!

The tutus bounced and flounced as
the gobble-uns shook with disgust.

"Let's get out of here!" they cried.

The gobble-uns turned and tore past
Pearl, Olive, and
Tweet, straight
out of the cave.

"What about our apples?" Pearl asked.

"Never mind," said Olive, fanning the air. "They'll be all stinky and covered in gobble-un germs."

Pearl stared at the ogre girl. Olive refusing to look for food? Never, ever had this happened before.

They hurried after the gobble-uns.

Outside, they watched the gobble-uns jump around, trying to pull off the pink tutus. They ran along, bouncing and kicking and tumbling over.

The apple tree shook and shuddered as they ran past. Then apples started falling from the branches.

"Apples!" cried Tweet.

With the gobble-uns gone, the three friends sat down in the forest and helped themselves to an apple feast! The apples were juicy and there wasn't a gobble-un germ to be seen.

Olive lay back on the grass. "I'm so full," she said. "I couldn't eat another apple!"

"Gobble-uns ran!" shouted Tweet. She laughed so hard she fell over an apple.

Pearl smiled. She was magical Pearl again and it felt good. She tossed and wiggled in delight.

Then . . .

SPLOT!
SPLOSH!
SPLOOSH!

"Oops."

MORE MAGICAL ADVENTURES COMING SOON!

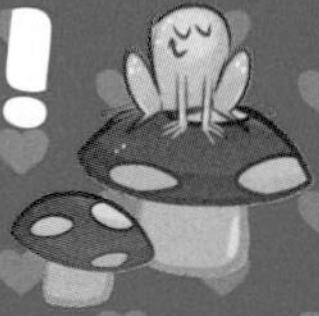

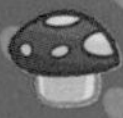

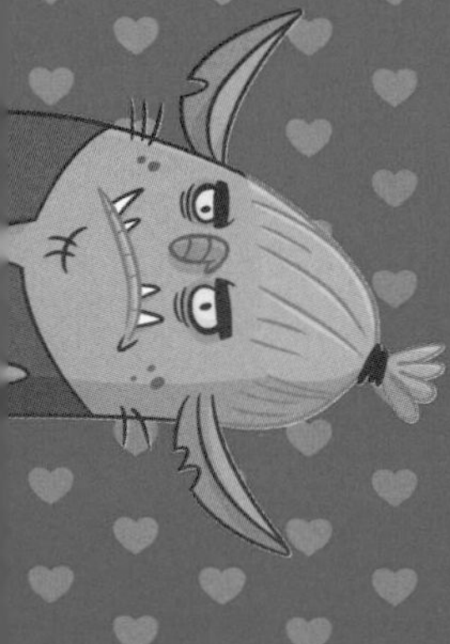

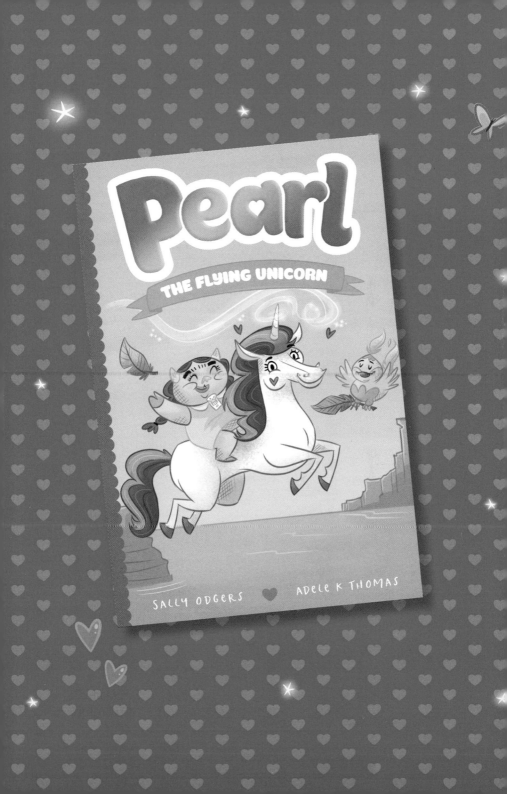

SALLY ODGERS was born in Tasmania, Australia, in 1957, and has lived there ever since. Sally began writing as a child, and her first book was published in 1977. More than 250 books have followed, including *Good Night, Truck*. She is married to Darrel Odgers, and they have two adult children, James and Tegan. Darrel and Sally live in a house full of books, music, and Jack Russell terriers.

SALLYODGERS.WEEBLY.COM

ADELE K THOMAS is a Melbourne-based illustrator, director, and art director with over ten years of design experience in animation production, TV, children's books, advertising, and apps.

ADELEKTHOMAS.COM

Thank you for reading this
Feiwel and Friends book.
The friends who made

THE MAGICAL UNICORN

possible are

Jean Feiwel, Publisher

Liz Szabla, Associate Publisher

Rich Deas, Senior Creative Director

Holly West, Senior Editor

Anna Roberto, Senior Editor

Kat Brzozowski, Senior Editor

Alexei Esikoff, Senior Managing Editor

Kim Waymer, Senior Production Manager

Erin Siu, Assistant Editor

Emily Settle, Associate Editor

Foyinsi Adegbonmire, Editorial Assistant

Sophie Erb, Associate Designer

Lindsay Wagner, Production Editor

Follow us on Facebook or visit us online at mackids.com.
Our books are friends for life!